TELL ME THE REASON WHY YOU LEFT

BASED ON THE LOST DIARY OF A TRUE LOVER

JAYANTH KASHYAP

ISBN 979-888555677-4

This book is dedicated to all those who have lost their
loved ones

Contents

Foreword

Tell me the reason why you left is a hauting experience of a true love story that was based in an urban setup. This is the story of everyday life and events that has occurred and forgotten. After finding this diary in a vacated and haunted house. I was curious to know what accounts would writer leave behind. This is a short diary based novel which has probably no starting or ending part but leaves the reader wanting for more. Some love stories have no endings.

Preface

This is my first book as an independent author. I wrote this memoir to find the little lost moments that every lover would leave behind. I wrote this book to explore what has been lost. I wrote this book to remind people who they have become after loosing their love.

CHAPTER I

It just took a second to fall in love!

It takes a moment to fall in love and a lifetime to forget.

Myself Jaineel and this is my life story. I had many crushes all my life and it was a Monday morning and I was in my school wearing the school uniform i.e. white shirt and brown trousers, looking tidy. By the way, I was the class representative, Oh! Sorry, this story begins from my 8th grade.

I sat on the last bench, my science teacher explaining the distribution of atoms, it was the month of May, I looked outside the classroom to find the bright shining empty corridors of my beautiful school. I continued to enjoy the bright sunny afternoon after lunch. I closed my eyes feeling a bit drowsy. "Excuse me, Mam," She said

The voice which I would probably hear every day for the next half-decade, the voice that still lingers in my ears even today. "Can I borrow the duster please"? I woke up from my trance to discover who this lady was!

I remember this line from a poem from my school days.

"So sweet a face, such Angel grace, in all that land had never been!

She looked bright! Probably I Fell in love or maybe not, I may have fallen in love with her chubby cheeks and goli vada pav eyes! Love, at first sight! It was a fountain of emotions and sweet pain in the heart. I need her for life, I need her forever.

Maybe I fell in love! Falling in love is short, Forgetting is forever!

If love was a crime, then I would be convicted for life for the crimes I did. I assumed what if she becomes my everything in life. The next step was to know her name class & section.

A few days later I started to collect all her details. I asked one of her classmates who was my best friend then. " Appi can I know about her". Appi probably was in love with me, she didn't disclose any details, it was time to show some courage to get to talk to her.

What a coincidence if I say, The school principal and authorities arranged for an educative trip to a botanical garden to study plants, wow! So kind of them.

The day of the trip came, we were in this botanical garden studying varieties of plants! Sorry, she was observing plants and I was observing her. My cunning friend Darshan, dragged me to talk to her. She stood in front of the sun, It looked like a Maniratnam movie scene! I went to her to express my love, said to her " Hai, Myself Jai...She stopped me and replied "Hi brother! Nice to meet you" and left. I stood broken.

It was our *first* conversation, it broke my heart. I walked from that botanical garden to home crying. Never before was my heart so heavy! Every step that I took spoke to me, it said " I need her".

I was the class representative and a popular student in my school days, her silence and her don't give a damn attitude on me did affect me. My ego wasn't hurt but I was ready to pour my love, energy, and time and anything more she would ask for? I was ready to shell out.

Being a student volunteer in my school, I took charge of her class to monitor during that botanical garden visit. I ensured that she would be alone for a few minutes so that I could express my emotions, but she called me Brother, did she even realize what damage it caused? Maybe not or maybe was this a sign of how our future would be?

Just before the morning of the botanical garden visit, I alongside a few of my friends planned everything and made suitable arrangements so that I can talk to her. We even drew a map of where all places do we visit and what place exactly she could be alone with her friends and where there would be a no teacher zone! All that she did for our plan was a flop show!

She just left

She never told me why She left! Never did I ever ask why she left.

CHAPTER II

Permanent love for an Impermanent Life

Two years passed by and I was in my 10th grade, in charge of hoisting the school flag on the 15th of August, Independence day. As soon as I entered the school, my eyes looked for her, I could see her in a corner seated. She gazed at me! It was morning 8 AM, that freshness of her sight and the morning weather! I can't describe how deeper she was pulling me into her love tornado

The news of my love for her spread throughout the school like wildfire. Finally, she knew that I did like her through her friends. I sang the National Anthem with pride and came back to my seat, I saw her, and she for the second time looked at me with a gentle smile and disappeared. Does she love me ? or maybe not?

All love stories have seniors who help, mine too, her name was Pavithra, a close friend of my almost love or I can call a crush. Pavithra called me " Jai... come near the computer lab it's an emergency". I ran, I saw her standing alone, nobody around.

I could feel my heart throbbing, my breath got deeper. I wasn't prepared to face her. I was afraid or excited. I gathered all my courage "If you are free, can we take a walk home today?". I said Omg! What did I just say?

She stared me for a moment, I wasn't prepared for another NO, She said "Yes". For the first time, I felt the need to protect her, care for her and hold her palms. She climbed down the stairs from the computer lab. Broke her slippers! Waah! What timing!

She did feel sorry seeing me. I wished I could hold her hands and walk her home. I couldn't because I wasn't officially her love yet.

She had to take an auto home and cannot accompany me to walk. Thus began the role of her unofficial guardianship. Maybe I decided to be possessive or I was always one. I called the Autorickshaw, she sat inside, staring at me. I wanted to talk a lot to you, my eyes told her. She spoke "I want this relationship of ours to be permanent, if it's temporary let's stop it today!" and she left, rickshaw driver smiled.

Never did I ask her why she left or did she tell me the reason why she left hurriedly!

CHAPTER III

Inter-Caste Love

That evening was special; It was 2006 or 2005 I roughly remember the year. All I wanted to was to express my love for her. She didn't even allow me to propose her, she wanted a permanent relationship with me! There was a joy inside me, I couldn't sit or stop myself from smiling.

I soaked in the memory of what happened early in the day. It was time to make a permanent decision in this impermanent life. I didn't think much or maybe I should have given a thought. I geared up for the journey that would probably last for the next half-decade or more. I fell inside a journey that made me an obsessive lover, the journey that changed the course of life.

I called her landline phone number, which she sent me through her friends. Her mom spoke, I said "Aunty Can I talk to your daughter". Her mom didn't speak much, she said okay.

I spoke to her, "Can we meet tomorrow after school and take a walk home?". She agreed! The next day was exciting, I am sitting in the class for the school timings to get over. Butterflies in the belly.

I stood next to the school gate, there was a medical shop, where all my friends and teachers would stand. I waited there, she didn't turn up even after 10 minutes after the school time.

I went inside, she stood at her class, alone she stood. I went " I am waiting," I said, she nodded her head and came out. She wasn't a normal daring girl, she was timid and probably expected me to be her side at every step of life, I assumed.

Our first walk had started, the journey of a thousand miles began with a single step. I looked deep into her eyes! *I still look deep into people's eyes if I adore them*; she never looked deep into my eyes entire our journey.

I spoke, "I'm hungry, can we eat something"? That was our *first* supper! We did want to speak a lot but we didn't. Butterflies still flying around, she was dominant & emotional little girl; we knew that our love is not going to be an easy one. Inter caste love stories in our household were still a stigma. I did convey to her that we would face issues in the future, she knew it well. She said she wouldn't leave me AT ANY COST.

When the blanket of love is wrapped around, the whole world seems blind.

After completing the supper, I realized that my pocket was empty, she paid our first bill. It would be wrong on me if I don't acknowledge the fact that entire relationship, she almost maintained the running cost of our expense.

I called the auto again, we both sat inside, I realized I was becoming possessive, which today I would tell people is a wrong trait. Inside the auto, for the first time, she held my palm tight! I'm shocked; unable to know what to do, I kept mum! She kept her pillow-woven teddy bear cheeks on my shoulder and said "You never gave me an answer whether our relationship would be permanent or temporary?"

I held her palms tight! "No matter what or who comes in between us, I shall be with you"

I dropped her home, I walked from her home to mine because I couldn't afford to spend the money if any other day she asked me to drop her; soaking in what promise I just made. Maybe I got committed, or maybe not. *When her destination arrived* she never looked back.

She left..

I didn't ask her why she left so soon. Never did She ever reply

CHAPTER IV

Guardian for Life

We joined the same college for pre-university studies; I honestly had no idea, why we both ever joined that Institute. One bad day of our love life finally arrived, probably the one problem every Indian boyfriend would face is the need to protect his girl from the uncultured lot.

She was walking from her house to college, while on the way she was eve teased by a group of A**H****.

She called me immediately crying on the phone of what had happened. My blood boiled, I rushed towards her location with few of my school friends, who apparently are still my friends we carried cricket bats, hockey sticks and wickets, we were going for a gang war.

She stood there crying. It broke me into pieces. I could never see my girl in that position ever again.

Unfortunately, we couldn't find them but my girl stood sobbing. I am shy from nature, but for the first time, I hugged her. Now was my time to decide my life. She asked "Can you please be with me always. I didn't think much I said, "Yes, I will".

Maybe I should have given it a thought. This might sound crazy but every single day for the next 5 years of college life, I picked her up and dropped her. No joke. We fought some days, we were caught with our relatives on some days, but my service for her never stopped.

One day in the first semester this happened, I never had the practice of carrying a lunch box, she entered my class suddenly handed me her lunch box filled with delicious food, told me to eat and return the box. It bought tears to my eyes; she loved me deep I understood that she was the most innocent creature I ever found. This practice of lunch continued for probably the next 3 years. Over love story in college became a role model. Teachers knew us but never objected to us because I was a distinction holder in my academics, she wasn't too studious but not too bad in academics.

CHAPTER V

Moments are gone but Memories Remained

That evening I felt not so good, as they say when you don't feel better something bad happens.

I received a call for my landline. She spoke, "Please meet me evening at 6 O clock its urgent, come to my house street corner and stand, I shall meet you". She said this in a tense voice and cut the call!

My heart started racing, Probably the first time I realized that loving isn't an easy affair anymore. My mind had a billion negative thoughts. I prepared for my own illusions of questions and answers. What if her parents came? What if her relatives bought weapons to kill me? I'm sorry but I couldn't stop these thoughts. The problem with inter-caste love is there is always a portion of that insecurity in the mind. Spending time till 6 o clock was hell.

It was finally 6 O clock, I had a friend who had bought a red color *deo vehicle* that was robbed elsewhere (I didn't honestly know it was robbed), I rode the vehicle so fast that evening and stood at the place where we finally had to meet.

Being anxious, worried and panicked. She came running towards me, she held my jacket collar and said "my parents want me to get married soon," she said. Hardly touched 18 years of age, not even legal age for men to get married, no proper qualification or sufficient money, what courage could I give her?

I said " I can take care of you only if you can wait for me a few years more... else our relationship....might..." I didn't end my conversation, she hugged me. I was shocked at what happened. She smiled and said, "Nobody is getting me married, I just felt like seeing you, so I made this plan".

I abused her not openly but in my mind. Probably I didn't like her way of doing this or maybe it was cute for her and not for me. I didn't realize it. Now should I feel happy because we hugged or because you gave an Instant relief. I wanted to speak I didn't. She left running back, she left.

While I was returning home with the robbed deo I was caught by the Inspector of traffic himself. He did ask me for a Driving License, Insurance and Vehicle documents. I opened the vehicle storage only to realize it was empty. *When things go out of hand I strongly believe truth should prevail.*

I spoke to the police " Sir, my girl was in trouble, I didn't know what to do, so I had to borrow the vehicle of one of my friends to meet her immediately, I absolutely have no license or insurance paper neither". Police stared at me for a long time and said "you can go now". I left.. The great escape,

Only after I was returning the vehicle to my friend did I realize that the vehicle was stolen and my so-called friend was running an illegal business, I wonder what if I was caught that day ? never mind she left..

CHAPTER VI

Every Love has a Rainy Story

Second-year of the graduation, one of our mutual friend, her name Sneha, her sister was getting married that day night, me and her, we both decided to attend the celebrations. It was 7 p.m., we reached the marriage hall. We stood together, it felt so couple!

We dreamt of being this eye-catching couple wherever we go, we were actually the gorgeous couple. We wished the newlywed couples all the very best. We did dream of our marriage that day, the enchanting part of every love story is that couples dream too much. Probably way too much.

It was 9 PM before we finished our wedding dinner, we smelt the cold breeze flowing across.

The ambiance around was chilled up. I did hear the thunders, she knew that I always feared the sound of thunders; she took my palm and held it tight. I loved that moment. The best part of being in true love is that you don't need to explain what you fear and what you don't; unfortunately, that is the worst part too!

I decided to drop her home as fast as possible, I said "Chiku let's go home before it rains, (Oh yeah, I called her Chiku because her cheeks were too fat). Her mom called me before we started the vehicle "Please don't drench her in rain, she suffers from acute asthma. Make sure you reach home within fifteen minutes". I saw the clock it ticked 9.15 PM already, I did what every possessive boy would do for her love, removed my puma jacket, and made her wear it. Put the helmet on her and started driving back home. Bangalore rains! Aha! What timing, we just started to drive there you go beauty, it poured, it rained like never before. My visibility went blurred,I could hardly see roads or where I was driving.

Even today when it rains. It etches the moments spent, *moments are gone but memories remained.*

I tried to be a hero, drove fast as I could, in real life heroism don't work. My vision started to blur, droplets of rain were so heavy, it hurt my face. I smiled!

All I could recollect was I was protecting my girl. She screamed "Stop the vehicle". I stopped. She suddenly took her helmet off, made me wear it, I refused. She worried I was hurt, I worried she would be drenched. I even thought my would-be mom-in-law would also appreciate my care for her daughter if I protected her from rain.

I stopped my vehicle in between the heavy rains, made her wear it again. She jumped off the vehicle, I shouted "Shut up and wear". "*You shut up!*" She replied, that was the first instance all my life I saw her raising her voice, she continued "Would you still love me, if I am not alive from tomorrow onwards". I wanted to hug her, I don't remember why I didn't and maybe I was too shy. I still am, I spoke "Can we go home please, its hell raining here". She was the most stubborn cute lady I ever met. " I would die but not leave you" I shouted in the middle of heavy and thunderstruck rain. She smiled sat back wore the helmet. Her home came, her mom saw us both, her mom saw us like I was a villain. She ran towards home not realizing that I need both a helmet and a jacket. She ran fast, closed the gate and went inside , never saw back. I wanted to ask her why she left, not to be seen back ever again.

CHAPTER VII

Love is Blind, Money Isn't.

I am pretty sure; I could explain the depth of our love story until now. I had a severe cash crunch. The maintenance of my love life was getting expensive. I had to travel early morning to her house every day by auto, pay auto fare and my father wasn't printing money in RBI nor was I son of Ambanis. "Necessity is the mother of invention". I decided to start my own part-time business. It was the year 2012 around, the boom was *Sim cards* and SMS! I encashed this business, collected a lot of ID proofs of my friends, purchased *free Sims* with *fancy mobile numbers*. That was the crazy era of fancy numbers like 999,666,333, and obviously 143's ! I sold all the free *SIM CARDS* I took for the exorbitant price of rupees five hundred and thousand.

I did all these to meet the running expense of my love life. I didn't feel sufficient no matter how much I earned until I realized that my business was semi-illegal. Never the less I immediately received calls from the local police station warning me to sell *sim cards*! I felt so good not because I received calls from the police but my business model started attracting enemies too! I didn't put much effort to be friends with many in the college, but I still have two or three best people with me event today. Pavan was my legal advisor, love consultant, life coach. I always did say to pavan that if he ever was a girl I would marry him and he was so understanding.

Pavan warned me many times that my over-the-board possessive love ship was titanic and would definitely sink one day! I never listened to anyone. Every boy would definitely have a best friend behind him who would guide him or be with him during the most distressing times! Unfortunately, our pavan's love story was one-sided.

Ganesh was one more hard-working, soft, and most gentle-hearted person, many underestimated his skills and humility. I only wish people respect the humble persons around. Coming back to my love expenses, I started one more business of selling crazy mobile pouches, arm mobile band-like pouches. I purchased them near K R Market at rupees fifty-odd and sold them again at a few hundred rupees! Due to the poor quality of my products I soon lost my customers and also market.

She was this Oriflame product agent selling products! She was managing our expenses better! All our expenses were for auto and petrol! Not that we roamed about too much, but still the modern century love required enough cash.

CHAPTER VIII

If bunking was an ART I was Picasso and she was my Paint!

I was dominant and possessive, she was more. Down the line, in life, we both realized this over-the-board protection and possessiveness was hurting us both. *No matter how much you love a bird, you cannot put it in a golden cage and make it happy.* We attended the college regularly for two hours every day and on some rare occasions three hours. It so happened one semester, I attended a lecture on financial management only to realize that the professor is seeing me for the first time. I felt bad, in love, while in love there is always an inner fight to attend the class to justify the money paid by the parents or to justify the love. I tried to balance but on most occasions, I was off-balance.

Our break time was at 11.30 AM, every time I stood near her classroom, a few of her friends would signal her that I came. She was so diligent in packing her bag and we together would walk off! Bunk like a king was our art, she was my apt princess! We never roamed around but we didn't want to miss our time talking to each other and building a future of our own. There were days I promised to take her out on a long drive and there were days I didn't want to bunk. We fought but we stayed.

In life I always felt the need to listen to our gut feelings, it always says the right things. One fine evening we roamed all around the city searching for some chocolates and gift items. I returned home and told my parents that we had a special revision class, so, I was late.

My Parents apparently had visited college that entire day

and waited for me to turn to college!

My class teacher had informed, I would bunk regularly and roam around with a girl from the next class, every day! Everything was fine until the parents start interfering.

The most you can trust someone in your life is always your parents & when they lose confidence in you, it's hell! I honestly didn't want my parents to feel bad about me, but I couldn't stop what was happening around me.

As they say, for all the bad things that happen in the world, mobile is the sole reason! My mobile phone got seized, trust me, today I feel that was the best thing my dad did, but I couldn't realize it then. It's very humiliating when friends and classmates get to know that you have fucked up your life! Trust me nobody cares. But there's always a friend who stands with you no matter what, they don't help you to come out of the situation but definitely stand by you when you are at crossroads. They were Pavan & Ganesh! After two days of isolation finally, I got the phone back, I did call her back, probably I was more worried about her than my life!

BUT SHE LEFT..

CHAPTER IX

It started to Saturate

While traveling one day in the final year of my college life, I kept her purse and belongings under my leg in a two-wheeler. After I stopped at her house I realized I had lost her wallet and belongings which had her passport, driving license, money and important documents!

It took me the next 2 weeks of college to roam around with her to get her problem fixed! That day she said, "You love me so much, that I am starting to feel suffocated". Was she joking? Maybe not.

My messages started to lose their relevance, "Love you" didn't mean love. I lied, a lot, most of the time she did too. I probably took too much of her space that we barely realized that it leads to saturation or may be suffocation. I don't know maybe possessiveness is a killing trait but tastes very sweet.

The one-time rudeness, which looked cute is now no cuter. I didn't like it. She didn't too. The blame game starts for every problem. I never blame her for what happened then, probably I thought I wasn't caring or loving enough, but today I realize, *the syllabi of love weren't my version of what I thought love to be.* Long drives that we took felt like I was a driver.

The artistic scoop I had was no more found. The extrovert me is long forgotten. Maybe she also altered a lot for me or for us. I cared for everyone, I still do, probably then I stopped. After half a decade of being in love, I stopped expressing myself, had occasional panic attacks, sometimes anxiety or unknown fear lurking around.

I panicked to talk to people, at times I stopped and realized what have I become? What have we become?

CHAPTER X

MARCH 5th

It was time for us to sit, talk to each other and rediscover ourselves, we were now graduates, the life which was filmy few years back wasn't filmy and rosy anymore. Love took a toll. I need space she mentioned quite a few times. She insisted on me rediscovering myself for our better future.

I was about to join a company for a job, she insisted that I join a better company soon so that we can talk about our marriage proposal soon in our house. I was in dilemma, I wanted to study more. Maybe I was selfish, we all are, being bought up in middle-class families, we blindly believe higher education is the cushion for life risks. I insisted that I would want to study higher, she should too. She wasn't keen on studying higher. I joined higher studies, she didn't. I didn't know where to meet her daily. I was her guardian all the while.

My hands felt tied, I couldn't help, we still met few times, but wasn't enough. She stopped the daily messages, or the message quantum got reduced by half. Calls became occasional. I got used to " had lunch", "had dinner", " text me when you reach home". These messages became redundant. I had just purchased my bike, but she wasn't too keen on it.

One not so fine day, we met at a small pizza place, neither did I wanted to eat pizza nor she. We still sat there to order. I can barely remember what conversation we had that day. I still try but couldn't grasp what she spoke. She insisted I talk to her mom soon. I wanted time, maybe the boy's like me, don't understand what was exactly was happening in her house.

She stopped texting me back after that day, or sometimes with rude replies! It didn't hurt, it killed. Phone calls went unanswered days together. Whatsapp was just booming, but she wasn't online. Days became unbearable, friends did tell me that she was getting married to someone else or maybe she fell in love again with someone else?.

The pain started taking its horrible wrath day by day, the longer you wanted to convince yourself that everything was okay, the shorter it took to realize that not all things are okay.

Loving you was temporary, but forgetting is forever!

By the time I received her call one day, I was panic-struck, dwindled and nobody realized what happened to me. She spoke, " *I want to show you the photo of the guy whom I'm marrying to, would you want to see?"*. *It killed. My blood boiled, my heart burnt!* She continued " *I do not want you in my life anymore"*. I spoke " *Okay"*.

The call got cut, I saw myself in the mirror, my eyes wet, my face looking pale, a big lump in my throat shouting to cry. It suddenly seemed weird. I didn't realize what happened.

A few days later my phone didn't buzz the way it used to buzz, days passed, hardly a few friends made. My parents didn't know what had happened. No messages or calls. I sat, at a lonely park, I wanted to cry, I cried. I cried aloud. The watchman came, hugged me. It didn't feel better.

I became quiet, maybe forever, I never spoke to people as much as I spoke. The relationship did look empty and void. I envied all couples who got into love and got married. I worked 18 hours a day, some days more, I didn't want to let myself down, but it didn't feel okay.

I don't regret my time, my effort, or the care that I gave.
It was March 5th she left; she never did tell me why she left
or maybe she did! All I want to ask her once is
"TELL ME THE REASON WHY YOU LEFT".

The End

For more such books and articles based on real and true events follow the author Jayanth Kashyap on Facebook and Instagram.